For Janna, Olive, and all of the fearless women in my life.

VIKING
An imprint of Penguin Random House LLC, New York

First published in the United States of America by Viking,
an imprint of Penguin Random House LLC, 2021

LIBRARY OF CONGRESS CATALOGING-IN-PUBLICATION DATA IS AVAILABLE.

EST

Manufactured in Spain

ISBN 9780593202289

10   9   8   7   6   5   4   3   2   1

Book design by Doug Cenko and Jim Hoover   Typeset in Decor and Trend HM Sans
The illustrations in this book were created digitally.

VIKING IN LOVE

DOUG CENKO

VIKING

Stig was like most Vikings.
He loved fresh air, hearty stew,
and, of course, adorable kittens.

But unlike most Vikings,
there was one thing
Stig did not like . . .

THE SEA.

It's not like he was scared
of it or anything . . .

(Okay, maybe just a little bit.)

One day, as Stig was taking the kittens for a walk,
he saw the most fearless Viking he'd ever seen.

And she said the sweetest thing he'd ever heard.

He tried to respond, but before he could . . .

the sea swept her away.

That night, he couldn't sleep.
He had to get his feelings into words.

He wrote all kinds of super-mushy stuff and even added a little heart when he wrote her name, like this:

Stig returned to
the beach with a note.

He waited . . .

and waited . . .

and waited . . .

But there was no sign of her.

Just when he was about
to give up hope, he saw her.

But she was too far away . . .

Ingrid

Stig

He folded the note into the shape of a ship and let it sail . . .

But the waves returned it to him.

He folded it into the shape of a bird and let it soar . . .

But the wind returned it to him.

Stig could only think of one way to get the note
to Ingrid. And as much as he didn't want to do it . . .

He tied the note to a kitten . . .

But that didn't go so well either.

As he was apologizing, Stig saw one final
way that he could get the note to Ingrid . . .

He was determined.

The sea tried to knock him
back, but Stig pushed on.

He thought that he would be okay
as long as he held on tight . . .

But the sea wouldn't let him.

Stig was finally able to
hand Ingrid the note . . .

But the sea had ruined it.

He was crushed.
Stig felt just like the note looked.
That was, until he heard . . .

This time, the sea couldn't stop him.

Ingrid's note was the sweetest thing that Stig had ever read.

She even added little hearts, like this:

Stig and Ingrid were like most Vikings . . .
They loved fresh air, hearty stew, and adorable kittens.

And together . . .

they conquered the sea.